Copyright © 1999 by Nord-Süd Verlag AG, Gossau Zürich, Switzerland
First published in Switzerland under the title *Hase Hannes bringt die Weihnachtspost*
English translation copyright © 1999 by North-South Books Inc.

First published in the United States, Great Britain, Canada, Australia, and
New Zealand in 1999 by North-South Books, an imprint of Nord-Süd Verlag AG,
Gossau Zürich, Switzerland.

Distributed in the United States by North-South Books Inc., New York.
Library of Congress Cataloging-in-Publication Data is available.
A CIP catalogue record for this book is available from The British Library.
ISBN 0-7358-1058-3 (trade binding) 10 9 8 7 6 5 4 3 2 1
ISBN 0-7358-1059-1 (library binding) 10 9 8 7 6 5 4 3 2 1
Printed in Belgium

For more information about our books, and the authors and artists
who create them, visit our web site: http://www.northsouth.com

Harvey Hare's Christmas

By Bernadette Watts

North-South Books

New York · London

One frosty December morning, Harvey Hare the postman crawled sleepily out of his warm house.

On the ground lay a big pile of packages, letters, and cards—more mail than he'd ever seen before.

"Oh dear!" he cried. "Christmas is nearly here. But all this mail will never fit in my bag."

Squirrel heard Harvey's cry. He hopped up to Harvey and said, "What you need is a big basket."

Squirrel called the other animals to help.
They collected dry rushes and willow switches,
and in no time at all had woven a basket for
Harvey to carry on his back.

Harvey was very relieved. "Thank you, everyone!" he said.
Then he loaded all the mail into the basket, lifted it onto his
shoulders, and set off.

It was a cold day. The pond was covered in a thick layer
of ice. But the basket kept Harvey's back warm as he trudged
on his rounds.

By evening Harvey Hare was totally exhausted. He had never delivered so much mail before. But when he finally got home, there was an even bigger pile of Christmas mail sitting in front of his house.

"Oh dear, oh dear," he said with a sigh. "My basket isn't big enough for all of this!"

Two owls overheard Harvey and flew off to tell the other animals of his problem.

"How can we help him?" they asked.

Porcupine knew just what to do.

Harvey could not get to sleep for a long time that night.
And when at last he did fall asleep, he had a terrible dream:
letters and packages were raining down on him!

He woke up in a panic, shook himself, and went to the
door. He couldn't believe his eyes!

Outside, all his friends were at work. Some collected
wood; others sawed, hammered, and glued.

"What are you doing?" asked Harvey.

"We're building a cart for you," said Raccoon. "For the
Christmas mail."

Harvey was delighted. He started to gather the packages
and letters. Rabbit, Squirrel, and Porcupine helped.

"Good luck, Harvey!" the animals called as Harvey set out with his new cart.

"Thank you, dear friends," said Harvey Hare, and he went cheerfully on his way. When it began to snow, he put up his umbrella to protect the letters and packages.

He delivered the last letter to Hedgehog, who
invited Harvey in for a cup of tea. It was snowing
harder as Harvey headed home that afternoon.

Suddenly he heard a loud *crash!* behind him. A wheel had
caught on a root hidden by the snow, and the cart was smashed.
  "What a shame!" said Hedgehog. "It was such a nice cart."
  Disappointed, Harvey left the broken cart in the snow
and trudged home.

When he got there, a mountain of new Christmas mail awaited him.

Harvey told Raccoon about the broken cart.

"Doesn't matter. Doesn't matter," said Raccoon. "A cart is no use in snow. You need a big sled."

The animals worked all night, and the next morning
there stood the sled!

"It's wonderful!" said Harvey. "Thank you so much.
But now I must be on my way. Today is Christmas Eve!"

Harvey pulled and pulled, but the sled didn't move an inch.
"We'll help you," said Mouse, taking a seat on top.
The others pushed, with Harvey leading the way.

They trudged up a steep hill. And that's when it happened:
All the packages and letters fell off the sled and slid down
the hill.

Owl was the first to pluck a small package out of the snow.
"Why, this is addressed to me!" she exclaimed.

"And this is for you, Squirrel!" called Porcupine.

"And this is for you, Harvey!" said Squirrel.

Then they all laughed. Everything that lay around them
in the snow was mail on its way to them!

"Harvey doesn't need to deliver any of this," said Fox.

"Let's celebrate Christmas together right here," suggested Porcupine.

Everyone liked that idea. So while some of them handed out the packages and letters, others brought food and candles to decorate the fir tree. Then they all sat together and opened their Christmas mail.

"Merry Christmas, everyone!" said Harvey.

And the animals all replied, "Merry Christmas, Harvey!"